DATE DUE			
ILL 11-17-92			

DEMCO 38-297

Tales of Darkest America

TALES OF DARKEST AMERICA

BY

FENTON JOHNSON

The Black Heritage Library Collection

 BOOKS FOR LIBRARIES PRESS
FREEPORT, NEW YORK
1971

First Published 1920
Reprinted 1971

Reprinted from a copy in the
Fisk University Library Negro Collection

PS 3519
.O24
T1x

INTERNATIONAL STANDARD BOOK NUMBER:
0-8369-8926-0

LIBRARY OF CONGRESS CATALOG CARD NUMBER:
72-178477

PRINTED IN THE UNITED STATES OF AMERICA
BY
NEW WORLD BOOK MANUFACTURING CO., INC.
HALLANDALE, FLORIDA 33009

Several of these stories appeared originally in The Favorite Magazine and are gathered together as testimonials of the life of the race to which I belong.

FENTON JOHNSON.

The Story of Myself

I HAVE gone through the Valley of Despair groping for the light that would aid humanity and caring little for the means of obtaining sustenance. I have borne the taunt of being an idealist but somehow I enjoyed idealism since it was fire and food for humanity.

I struggled through school and through the university, my star the star of the Muse and my hope the opportunity to follow the star of the Muse. When my school days had faded I went South to teach those of the race to which I belong and after a year of abject poverty, not even receiving my meagre salary of forty dollars a month, I returned to Chicago and struggled to obtain a foothold in literature.

It seemed to me like trying to walk the Atlantic ocean to obtain recognition in the literary world and especially when one was attempting to present the life of the race to which I belong. After what seemed to be a hopeless struggle a woman of infinite kindness and sympathy gave my first collection of poetry the material form of a book called "A Little Dreaming," which brought me recognition from that very good friend of literature, Dr. Albert Shaw, Editor of the American Review of Reviews, and his remarkable literary critic, Jeanne Robert Foster.

I moved to New York and through the kindness of another I attended the Pulitzer School of Journalism at Columbia University and published privately two new volumes of verse, "Visions of the Dusk" and "Songs of the Soil." Both met with very enthusiastic reviews on the part of the press, and resulted in my return to Chicago and the beginnning of my struggle in journalism.

It was during the memorable struggle at Argonne Forest that I founded The Favorite Magazine. I had nothing save a meagre allowance from a relative but I was determined to have a magazine and conceived the idea that I could accomplish a large number of reforms and the creation of a new literature through a magazine of my own. I went without meals and postponed paying room rent until I had saved ten dollars and went to a printer whose heart was very large and paid the ten dollars as a deposit on my first issue.

Then I took a dummy and went among my friends and solicited advertisements. At night and during spare moments I wrote the material for the issue and followed that custom until recently. In addition to that I exhausted all the names in the English language for non de plumes to go on the different articles, short stories and poems I wrote for The Favorite Magazine.

It was about that time that I met the woman of my dreams and when one meets the woman of his dreams he marries that woman despite the obstacles that might lie in his path. Although I had a magazine that had nothing but determination and imagination to back it and seventy dollars a month to live on, I married. It was not long after that I had nothing but the seventy dollars to support myself and my wife because The Favorite Magazine died with everybody recognizing its death but myself and my friend, James H. Moody, who had been with me from the beginning of the struggle.

It seemed to me as if I was about to face the bankruptcy court because I had a nine hundred dollar debt staring me in the face and no means of liquidating it. Everybody including my family turned a deaf ear to my pleas to save The Favorite

Magazine, although there came appeals from many throughout the country that the magazine should be continued.

An aunt died during those dark days of mine and although her death is one I have mourned a long time I inherited a small sum from her and the name of it saved the magazine and saved me from bankruptcy. Mr. Moody and I renewed our campaign for advertisements and subscriptions and the same kind printer brought out the new Favorite Magazine.

I worked as hard as ever and struggled in every way to obtain funds for the purpose of meeting the deficit. One incident I can never forget as long as I live and that is the case of Conkling, Price, Webb & Company, a bonding firm that refused me surety bonds to draw from my aunt's estate so that I could save the magazine from an impending refusal on the part of the poorly paid printer. The only cause given me was "that colored people's estates were too risky."

After that the struggle was more intense than ever. I had no funds to develop a very young proposition and no means of obtaining funds. I was confronted also by the wave of radicalism that was trying to engulf the race to which I belong, but I refused to sell my soul to the agitators of Bolshevism and brought unpopularity to the magazine among a certain class.

When the estate was settled I made a journey to New York and after a speech on "The Co-operation of the Races" I founded The Reconciliation Movement. I used all the money I had in developing this movement which was to me not only the solution of the race problem but also the problem of law and order.

It has been dark days trying to make The Reconciliation Movement successful in a country that until this moment seems to care little for any movement of that sort. No one but myself and James Moody knows the suffering that I have undergone and how near I am to what all of us dread, starvation.

As I write this in the little furnished room that my wife and I call home, I wonder if the Reconciliation Movement is not a grand dream, The Favorite Magazine a foolhardy venture and I, myself a failure. I wonder if I was wise in trying to follow the star of the Muse in America or if I should have gone to England or even Paris and cast my lot where I would not have had to climb over the barrier of race.

I know that I am facing ruin and starvation. I know that my dream of a magazine is about to end in the cold gray awakening because of the heavy debt hanging over it and the lack of desire Americans seem to have for the reconciliation of the races. I know that my dream of success in literature is fading because every story I have ever offered a standard magazine has returned to my desk and even in the case of the Saturday Evening Post, one story, "The White Slave," returned the day after it was sent.

I have one consolation; and that is that I have lived for the highest good and that I have injured no man, woman or child. All I pray for is that my wife and James Moody will not suffer if this struggle should end in my passing to the other world.

Through the Valley of Despair

HROUGH the Valley of Despair I wandered until I saw shining as a halo, the moonlight, which is a balsam for all troubled souls. The moonlight is at the end of the Valley of Despair and is a bath of blessedness for all who will bathe in it.

O Psyche, come with me through the Valley of Despair and let us bathe in the moonlight forever and a day.

A Very Important Business Man

F you had seen him a few years ago you would have wondered who The Beau Brummell could have been; because at that time he was dressed as spectacularly as possible and carried a walking stick everywhere he went. His walk was the walk of a man who had the burden of a large business on his shoulders and judging by his conversation you would have thought so.

He said to me one day, at about the time this story opens, "I am certainly a busy man. I have to look after everything; I am not able to trust the details to anyone except my private secretary and I have to watch him for fear he might take the business from me. And I'm suffering for lack of space. It is terrible to jam a business like mine into one room, but it is so difficult to get office space now a days. I would be glad if I could get an entire floor. I could place the secretary of my company in one room, the treasurer in another and the Vice-President and General Manager in a suite of rooms adjoining my suite. Then I could have a place to discuss my business in private and a special room for my secretary and his stenographer. As it is my business is kept back because when I want to discuss something to a customer everybody is listening and taking my business out of my mouth. I would give anything if I could get a suitable place for my business. Have you any place to rent?"

I told him to come up to my office and that I would look over my list and see if I had anything that was according to his specifications. He accepted my invitation, and after we had gone over the list, which was large at that time, he decided that a building that I had on the main street of the city would be apt to meet his requirements. He asked if he could see the building and I replied in the affirmative. We went to the building in my car, I having the vision of acquiring a long and prosperous lease from a very prominent business man. When we reached the place my prosepective tenant was very critical and I never had any idea the building had as many faults as he pointed out to me.

"The upper room has too much light," he said. "It would blind my eyes. And the large room on the left of the main floor is entirely too dark. I am afraid the other rooms are too small for a business like mine. It is certainly a keen disappointment to me; I was hoping that I had at last found a place a little better than the one room office I have now. I suppose I'll run across something in a few days. I thank you for showing me this place."

In those days a real estate man was apt to meet with many disappointments, so I merely placed this incident on my list of disappointments. However, I noticed that Mr. Merriwell, for that was his name, did not leave his little one room office, as he called it, but continued to complain about his lack of space and how much business he could do if he could only get larger quarters. At that time I thought he was a very super-critical man and wondered if he would ever find what he wanted.

About a year later I had occasion to call at his office and discovered that it was sub-leased to a growing baking powder firm. He was not in and the members of the baking powder firm did not seem very much concerned about him. They were preoccupied, having all they could do to look after their own interests. I met the proprietor and as is my custom, I cultivated his friendship, having in view the fact that I might be able to rent to him when his business reached that extent.

The proprietor of the baking powder firm said that Mr. Merriwell was very seldom in the office and that when he was he sat at his desk writing letters that he never mailed. Often he would complain about how difficult it was to obtain stenographers and how many had disappointed him even though he had offered them very liberal salaries. Occasionally he would ask if he could have the office for a few minutes because he had something of importance to discuss with a prospective customer. The proprietor of the baking powder firm said that he would go out and that his clerks would go out also and that when they returned they would find the very busy Mr. Merriwell discussing typewriter ribbons with a typewriter salesman. Mr. Merriwell, however, would tell the other occupants of the room about a wonderful deal he had made and how near he was to a very spectacular fortune.

"All I will have to do," he would say, "is to sign my name to the cheques and watch my officials. I intend to raise the salary of my secretary—he is getting twenty-five dollars a week, but that's not enough, considering the high cost of living. I think I'll rent this building. I'll need the space for my offices and probably I'll take the stores downstairs, also." He would turn to the proprietor of the baking powder firm and in a confidential tone remark, "If you desire to do so, I would be glad to have your firm as an auxiliary of my firm. You could be an officer and receive a salary for your services. Will you excuse me? I have a very important conference downtown. If anyone comes in to see me tell him I'll be here after six o'clock."

The proprietor of the baking powder firm said that he happened to be downtown that afternoon and being hungry, he entered a restaurant and seated himself at the lunch counter. He was surprised to see Mr. Merriwell waiting on the customers and was somewhat disconcerted when by chance Mr. Merriwell asked him what he desired. When Mr. Merriwell saw who he was he became slightly confused but quickly recovered his presence of mind and said in a very confidential tone:

"The proprietor of this restaurant is a very important stockholder in my firm and I'm assisting him during the rush. I came down here to see him regarding the proposition I was talking about with you this afternoon and noticing that he was short of help I offered to aid him though I know very little about waiting." And with that he left the proprietor of the baking powder firm and someone else brought the latter his order.

About a month or so later the proprietor of the baking powder firm came into my office and asked me if I had any offices to rent in that district of the city. He said that his facctious landlord had served him a notice to vacate before the tenth of the next month, because he needed the entire office for his own business. In two or three days I managed to secure an office for the proprietor of the baking powder firm and before the week was over the proprietor of that firm and his clerks had moved into it and they had begun the operation of their business as if nothing had happened.

It was not so with Mr. Merriwell. He came rushing into my office, following the removal of his tenant and pounding his fist on the railing in my outer office he shouted, which was something unusual for him to do. (He always spoke in a confidential tone.)

"What is the matter with that man who had the baking powder firm in my office? I tell you I'm going to get the law on him. I was helping him along and at the moment that he was beginning to make something for himself he moved out without even letting me know that he was intending to move. Nobody can get the best of me; I know too much about business. I've been in business all my life and there isn't anyone yet who has been able to put anything over on me."

I smiled and asked him why he had come to me about the matter he was discussing so impetuously. Mr. Merriwell lowered his voice, leaned over my shoulder and whispered "I want somebody to know what a scoundrel that man is and I thought this was the best place to secure witnesses. You know you have as busy an office as I have and I can advertise that rogue in your office better than in anybody else's." And with that he left my office scowling and his beadlike eyes flashing fire.

I went back into my private office and smiled. I had begun to see him as a man who was playing the role of a very important business man somewhat as Jacques Lebaudy played the role of the Emperor of the Sahara. The next day I happened to drop into the office of the proprietor of the baking powder firm, who seemed to be worried over something. I asked him what was the trouble and he replied, "Mr. Merriwell was in yesterday afternoon and said that he intended to put you in jail for attempting to have me break my lease with him. I couldn't pacify him nor could I explain to him that I moved subject to his order."

I smiled and asked my worried tenant if he had a copy of the order. He said he had and showed it to me. It was written on the back of a business card and had the very pompous signature of F. P. Merriwell. I explained that he need not fear his former landlord.

I called on Mr. Merriwell that evening and asked him if he intended to place me in jail. He feigned surprise at such a question and asked me if his secretary had said that. "His secretary," he said, "was one who was always doing something against him. In fact, his secretary was the cause of the baking powder firm moving."

"Now, my good friend," he added, "I have nothing against you. I am the best friend you have; but as for that scoundrel who runs that baking powder firm, I'm going to put him in jail. I have the goods on him. Nobody can put anything over on me. I'm too good a business man to be deceived by one like him. Do you know how much I did for him? Often I would lend him money and even gave him stock in my company and let my secretary work for him. Ingratitude is a terrible pill to swallow. But I'll get him! Yes, I'll get him!"

I showed him his order for his tenant to move and told him if he attempted legal proceedings on such a basis it would result in something disastrous for himself. "Mr. Merriwell," I added with a nod of my head, "It is best to let the milk that is spilled lie on the ground because it is impossible to recover spilled milk. This gentleman is spilled milk. Either get new milk or do without any at all."

I left the office and regarded the incident as closed. A few weeks later I heard that Mr. Merriwell had at the request of his landlord retired from business and in order to occupy his hours of leisure, which were twenty-four in a day, he was waiting table in the restaurant where he had taken the order of the proprietor of the baking powder firm.

A Woman of Good Cheer

SAW her the first time in a little town not far from St. Louis. She was at that time a middle aged woman, very erect in her carriage, dusk brown of complexion, clear eyed, gifted in the ability to smile and very alert in her walk. She was living in a little cottage on the outskirts of the town and was at that time very busy in the little garden that she had planted in the rear of her home.

"How lovely your garden looks" I remarked.

"Won't you have some of my sweet peas?" she asked me without even waiting for my answer. Before I knew it she had clipped me a nosegay of the loveliest sweet peas I had ever seen.

"Do you raise these flowers merely for your own enjoyment?" I asked.

The lady smiled such a smile as only she could smile.

"I raise them for whomsoever should desire them. Won't you come in and have tea with me?" was her reply.

I could not refrain from accepting her invitation. I went in the house and was seated in a cool shaded parlor. I noticed the walls were decorated with the pictures of the seventies, chromos of quaint old figures in jerseys and creaseless trousers, and the chairs were the old fashioned hair stuffed plush chairs. The table was decorated with a Bible and an album and the scarf that covered the table was embroidered presumably by her own hands. I felt that I already loved my hostess. I thought of her as a lovable woman who had cherished that that her mother had left behind. I longed to know more of her and consequently was glad when she returned with a pitcher of lemonade and a plate of golden wafers.

We spent a very pleasant afternoon. She told me that she had never married but had spent a large part of her life in trying to make it pleasant for all those with whom she came in contact. She was very fond of the books that had been created during the Victorian period and during her conversation she recited quotations from many authors that we of today consider standard. She was very religious in her views and expressed her love for the town because of its freedom from everything of the nature of intoxicating liquor.

The door bell rang several times during our conversation. My hostess, whose name was Alice Winston, would go to the door and would laughingly greet a roguish youngster who wanted a cookie or a flower from her garden. Miss Winston would always grant the request with a smile and would be cheered by the sign of pleasure on the face of the child.

To me she said, "It would certainly be a very miserable world without a child to give something to that would cheer him. I wish the world had more children. I am very fond of children. I only wish that there were more in the world. I am very fond of doing something cheerful for every child that I see."

When I left her the moonlight was glowing on the little garden. She herself was standing by the gate, the spirit of contentment on her face. I will never forget the picture she presented as she stood there, a good angel in a world harassed by the spirit of worry and unrest. Sometimes I think the angels were standing around her, guarding her as the angel guards the Garden of Eden. After I had gone a space I heard her singing a tune which was very popular about twenty years ago and which was very sentimental. She had a very melodious voice that with training might have equalled the voice of a concert singer and have given her a large measure of wealth, according to the standards of a materialistic community.

The next time I saw her was in St. Louis a few years later. She had changed considerably. The hair had grown almost white, the skin had become dry and parched and the walk was not as erect as it was the other time I saw her. But the smile lingered on her lips and there was a sparkle in the eyes that reminded me of a sparkle I had seen in the Mississippi river on a summer's evening. It was the same Alice Winston, the same gentle woman, who was able to see the beauty of life wherever she might be and under whatever circumstances she might be placed.

"I am so glad to see you," she said as she lingered to talk with me.

She told me she was working in a social settlement somewhere in the heart of the city. She said she had realized her aspiration—that of working for others. She was receiving a nominal salary but was very happy despite the struggle to live on the small amount she was granted for the large amount of work she was doing.

"If you could see the happiness on the faces of those for whom I am striving to give the best within me, it would do your soul good," was the way she expressed her satisfaction with her reward.

I inquired about her after she left me and discovered that Alice Winston was considered an angel of mercy throughout that portion of the city. The poor and needy were very fond of her and the children loved her as they love the patron saint of Christmas. The people always spoke of her in reverence and hoped that she would be with them for many years.

But this hope was not to be accomplished. A few days after I saw her on the street, I was visiting a hospital that belonged to the race that she belonged to and saw in the charity ward the figure of Alice Winston, cold in death. The smile lingered on her lips and the sunlight played on her temples as a halo in death.

The Sorrows of George Morgan

EORGE was desired to stay after school, and naturally his heart was filled with wonder. What had he done to deserve such a fate, so terrible to a child of ten? Had he not been diligent in his studies? Had he not recited correctly his history lesson and his grammar lesson, and even surprised Miss Anderson in his mastery of percentage and fractions? It was true he had pulled Genevieve's golden curls, but golden tresses were always alluring to his big brown eyes, that were constantly searching for beauty. Perhaps Miss Anderson was peeved at him for pulling Genevieve's curls and had therefore ordered him in such severe tones to remain after the others had gone.

As he sat there, the sunlight playing on the dark brown of his face, Miss Anderson, a prim woman, cast her cold gray eyes at him and in a tone sharper than the keenest knife, said: "George, I have kept you in for your own good. What I am going to tell you now, I hope you will remember as long as you live. George, you are not like the rest of these children. They are white, and you are merely 'a common darky.' You are as much beneath them as a chimpanzee is beneath you. In other words, you are inferior, and you should learn to keep the place of an inferior. Quit pulling Genevieve's curls; she's white and not made to associate with you. That is all, George; you may go."

George went, but the great knife of despair was cutting deep within him. As he walked home he thought of his teacher's cruel words, and his eyes filled with tears. "He was inferior," "a common darky." He was doomed to walk in a world outside of the world of those he played with at school and loved as all children love. Miss Anderson had rudely and decisively shut to him the great doors of human brotherhood. Would they ever open again? Would the world ever be the same? And to think that every place he would go he would be "A common darky" instead of a man, was bitter wormwood to a sensitive nature. Was life worth the living under such circumstances? Was it worth while to struggle, to suffer the defeats of life and to win, despite defeats, if his achievements were to be marked "Inferior?" What was there left for him that he should live and protect his life? Why not end it as he had heard of people ending their lives when the door of hope had been shut against them?

So at the tender age of ten, George contemplated that most hopeless of crimes, suicide, goaded to it by the foolish remarks of a school teacher who should have been careful of the soul of her charge. When he reached the little frame house that he knew and loved as home, George went up to his room, sat down on the the little white bed, and in his childish way planned a thrilling suicide. He would on the morning to come rush to the window of the school room, raise it, climb upon the ledge and let his swaying body fall to the ground. When the curious crowd surrounded him he would open his eyes and with the gasping breath of a dying child he would say, "Miss Anderson caused me to do it. She said I was not as good as the rest."

He cried a little and fell asleep. Sleep is the healer of wounds. God shifted to George the vision of an angel standing on the threshold of heaven, holding in his hand a scroll of parchment, and saying in a voice sweeter than the song of a humming bird, 'Be of good cheer, George! God loves all of us, black and white, poor and rich. Remember, George, God loves all of us."

When the vision vanished George awoke and rubbed his eyes, a new light on his countenance. "God loves all of us," so he was not "a common darky" in God's sight. He could forge ahead and God would reward him according to his merits and not the erroneous idea of race. He would keep his covenant with his Creator and demonstrate to the scoffers what "a common darky" could do.

The years have been spent. George has kept his covenant. He has worked hard, all the time fighting poverty and disappointments. Every time despair tried to fasten its fangs into him he would remember his childhood vision and work the harder. As he said often, God was his partner and he would not go against his partner.

After graduating from the College of Liberal Arts at the university, with honorable mention in history and economics, he accepted a professorship in one of the small Southern schools founded for one portion of the American people. With diligence he climbed into the Presidency of the school in less than three years, and became a gifted speaker in his community. The race question was usually his topic, since it is the topic closest to the hearts of those in the South.

It happened that the President of the United States was to speak at Vicksburg, the city not so far from George's school. It was during the Great War, and as a demonstration of good will a few Negro speakers were invited. George was among them, and a certain pardonable pride filled his heart. When his turn came George arose, faced the vast audience, and in a voice eloquent for its earnestness he pleaded the cause of his people. The hearers sat spellbound; here was a new Frederick Douglass, a new Washington, pleading for a despised race as only Demosthenes or Cicero could have pleaded.

He pictured the struggle of his race during the dark days of slavery. He pictured the dawn of emancipation that inspired the freed people to sing songs of Jubilee and to thank the God adversity had taught them to love and worship. He pictured the struggle of the reconstruction era and the great industrial striving of the newly made citizens of the leading republic of the world. He pictured the persecution they had undergone and the misunderstandings that they were accustomed to labor under and suffer. And as a climax he pictured the ready response they made to the call of the nation and humanity during the Great War, that turning point in the history of mankind. He told stories that caused the great auditorium to reverberate with laughter; in a kindly fashion he displayed to the world the rich humor that lay in that race. And in the same voice that had caused them to laugh hilariously he caused careless men and women to weep out of pity for a suffering people. With marked dexterity he played upon the passion strings of his hearers and stamped upon the hearts of the most prejudiced a strange sympathy for the black man.

And with simple but dramatic fervor he stretched forth his hands in suppliance and cried, "My friends, do not forsake us. We of the black race are working for you; work for us likewise. We will build for you Aladdin's palace in the desert of Sahara; build for us a secure place in the hearts of the American Nation. We do not ask for gold and diamonds, nor for the ease of a redeemed soul in the Paradise of Mohammed, but we do ask for a man's chance in a country designed for men."

The applause was long and loud. George bowed, but it was plain to see he was surprised. The world was conquered; it lay at his feet, he who had been despised by his teachers years before.

When George finished his address the President of the United States arose, rushed over to the bowing son of a suffering people and shook his hand vehemently. Raising his own hands aloft, the President demanded silence. "My friends," he said, "This night the Negro race has been given a new leader. There is nothing in this glorious old republic too good for this young man."

After the close of the meeting an old, dilapidated, gray-haired white woman pushed through the crowd congratulating the new Negro leader, and shook George's hand saying, "Don't you remember me, boy? I taught you when you were but a tot."

"Taught me?"

"Yes, I am Miss Anderson. You remember me now don't you?"

"I should say I do." There was a mischievous smile on George's face. "And do you remember the common darky?"

Miss Anderson turned away, tears in her eyes. Noticing the signs of repentance on the part of his aged teacher, George rushed up to her, put his strong hands on her weary shoulders and said, "Forgive me, Miss Anderson; I am sorry I hurt you. But the taunt has lived with me all these years. Tell me you are sorry."

Miss Anderson smiled faintly through the tears. "I'm sorry, George; I did wrong. But I am a changed woman now and I am glad that you didn't let what I said ruin you. You're launched on a splendid career and may God bless you."

And so with his arm guiding her, George escorted her to the President of the United States.

Trusting Providence

UMMER lingered in the lap of autumn. I, too, was lingering in a world that seemed anxious to forget me, so I could easily sympathize with summer. I was as shabby as summer was forlorn and my back was as bent as the backbone of summer. I had just as much money in my pocket as summer had in her pocket and you know how much money summer has in her pocket. My stomach was just as empty as the hollow of a tree and I fancied I could hear the bones of my stomach rattle.

I was wondering at the time where the poorhouse was located. I asked a policeman on the corner where I could find the poorhouse and he told me to go to his house, adding "there isn't a poorer house in the city." I thanked him and went on, not caring to reside at a house quite as poor as a policeman's house.

As I turned the corner I noticed a dog house. The dog who was enjoying free rent and free board looked at me and noticing how weak I was from hunger, invited me to pick a bone with him. I looked at the bone and looked at him and decided I would continue to starve.

I passed a restaurant. A man was flapping wheatcakes but he failed to flap any at me. The odor of food was very delicious and after filling my nostrils with all the odor of the food permissible, I went around to the rear with the hope of getting some of the scraps. But when I reached the spot I discovered that it was a very economical restaurant and that it never had any scraps. So I bewailed the spirit of economy that had come upon the world and decided that the only way a man could make an honest living was to hold up some one.

I wondered who I could hold up. I stopped a very busy footpad and asked him who I could hold up. He told me I could hold up my hands and said it very impressively with a 34 calibre, staring at me as rudely as possible. I wonder why 34 calibres stare at you; don't their parents teach them it isn't nice to stare at people? The footpad went through my pockets and finding them as naked as a new born baby, he gave me a ten cent piece and told me to purchase some carbolic acid at the nearest drug store.

Of course I didn't purchase the carbolic acid. I have never relished the taste of carbolic acid. I looked at the ten cent piece and wondered how much beefsteak I could purchase with it. I hurried back to the restaurant and after I had been seated I looked at the menu card and decided that the only thing I could purchase was a glass of water. I arose and handed the waiter the ten cent piece for his trouble. It is certainly fatiguing to dust off a chair and hand a menu card to a customer. Often I wonder how human beings can endure such sweatshops.

As I left the restaurant I noticed a woman as large as the Brooklyn Bridge was fainting, and crying, "Help! Help! Hold me up!" I was very gallant. I held her up for a dollar and a half and returned to the restaurant.

This time when the waiter offered me a menu card I told him not to exert himself so much, but merely order all he had in the kitchen, because I had a coming appetite. After the waiter had brought me the food and I had consumed over one-third of it he asked me when did my appetite leave. I told him that sometimes it didn't leave until the middle of next week and that I intended to satisfy it before I left the restaurant. The waiter became alarmed and whispered to the proprietor, who went to the telephone and called up the bankruptcy court. Before I was half through the sheriff had sold the restaurant and I left before the new proprietor had cleared away the old dishes.

So I had the dollar and a half in my pocket and enough food in my stomach to last me until they try the kaiser.

That night I accepted the hospitality of the city and slept on one of those nice green beds the city provides for its guests in that hotel known as Central Park. The bellboy, who wears a uniform of blue and a very shining star asked me what time I wanted to arise. I yawned and told him to wake me when the robins nest again.

He said, "Young man, the robins will never nest again." He convinced me that they would not by rapping me on the head with a little stick that he carries and treating me to the finest constellation of stars that I have ever seen. When I had finished counting the stars I discovered myself in a hotel that protects its guests with iron bars.

Yes, I am thoroughly convinced that Providence provides for all of us. You notice how well He provided for me—plenty to eat and a hotel where I was treated like a prince. I had plenty of guards when I was in that hotel and everyone was anxious that I should stay there. My friend, whenever you go to New York, trust Providence; if you trust any one else you'll go broke.

The Sorrows of a Stenographer

ELL isn't this a sorry sight? Here I arrive at the office and find that the boss has left a letter for me to typewrite. This is certainly a slave-driving office. Nothing but work, work, work, from morning until night. And I have so much to do. You know I haven't finished reading that novel, "The Last Kiss, or Was Mabel Fond of Chewing Gum?" It is a fine novel. The hero meets the heroine in the first chapter, takes her to supper in the second, gives her a spin in his Ford in the third, marries her in the fourth, falls in love with the bridesmaid in the fifth, and in the sixth the heroine meets the villain. I am breathlessly waiting to know what happens in the seventh chapter. The action is so rapid and realistic.

I like rapid novels, don't you? And I like to have them printed on good paper, also. My hair is unable to endure a bad quality of paper when I curl it. The last novel I read had such a bad quality of paper it was necessary for me to purchase a copy of **The Favorite Magazine** to get my hair back in shape.

I wonder why Charlie doesn't call me up. What's the use of a telephone in an office if your beau doesn't call you up at least three or four times a day? You haven't seen Charlie, have you? He's the sweetest boy alive; that's why I haven't paid much attention to the sugar shortage. And he's a swell dresser, also. He has the cutest coat I ever saw. It fits him just like my corset, and he's very particular about his hair. He goes to the same hairdresser that I go to and uses the same hair preparations that I use. I suppose that's why there's so much harmony of soul between us. And you should see the way he powders his nose; he does it more carefully than I do mine. He has a very gentle voice. I like gentle voices, don't you? I can't endure a harsh voice, especially in a man. But what I like about him best of all is the fact that he spends his money as freely as Henry Lincoln Johnson spent Lowden's. That's why I never cared for Apollo Belvidere; he has never had any money to spend.

What do you think of this high cost of living? Isn't it terrible? I hope that chewing gum doesn't go up. If it does, I won't be able to exist on my present salary. It's all I can do now to buy my supply of chewing gum, considering my meagre salary of twenty dollars a week. And I am told the price of rouge is going up. If it goes much higher it will be necessary for me to marry Charlie; he and I can share rouge between us and face powder also.

Marriage is economical for us women. I could wear Charlie's shirts and his shoes also, and spend his money. In fact, that's where I shine. I have studied closely the technique of spending money. I could spend "Brewster's Millions" in a minute and Rockefeller's millions in two or three hours at the most. I believe in keeping money in circulation. Keeping money in circulation is the salvation of our country, and I'm the greatest patriot in the world. I am always looking out for America's interests, especially when it comes to spending somebody else's money.

Papa says Charlie is wooden headed. That has made me more anxious than ever to marry Charlie, because wood is so valuable nowadays. Papa says Charlie's head is solid ivory. If it is solid ivory it would match with my bedroom suite, and I believe in matching things, even husbands. But what does papa know about husbands? He has never had any himself, and I believe only those who have had experience can judge, especially when it comes to marriage. I can read Charlie like a book; there isn't much to him either. He begins at the first chapter and ends on the second page. He's an unfinished work, a rapid action novel, and as I said I adore rapid novels. He calls me his lily-of-the-valley and I call him my Rose of Sharon. His face is red as a rose; he doesn't put enough powder on his cheeks to hide the rouge.

Charlie wanted to purchase me a diamond ring the other day. But I'm a very considerate girl, especially of a man I intend to marry. I told him to wait until diamonds became a little more expensive. I don't like him to waste his money buying diamonds when they're cheap. Cheap diamonds hurt my fingers and Charlie is very considerate about my fingers. That's why he never holds my hand; he's afraid he might squeeze it some time and hurt my fingers. The dear boy! How I adore him!

Excuse me a moment; the telephone is ringing. O pshaw! it was nothing but a fool customer. I don't see why customers desire to waste our valuable time. Here I am busy talking to you and that man called us up about a little hundred dollar order.

What was I talking about? Oh yes! It was about Charlie. Charlie's fond of looking into my eyes. He calls them the windows of my soul. But his face fell when I told him to put some panes on the windows. I don't care whether they're egg shell panes or common nose glasses.

That's a pretty waist you have on, dearie. Charlie has one just like it. I wonder if he bought it at the same counter that you bought yours.

Oh, there goes that telephone again. This is certainly a busy office. Why, hello Charlie! You will excuse me, dearie. I'll be talking for an hour or so. Charlie's my most important customer.

The Carnival

AM very fond of roving along State Street. I was roving along State Street on a very pleasant evening in May when the atmosphere was redolent with the warmth of the late spring. The street was crowded with the care free seekers of pleasure, everyone anxious for the goblet of the Goddess Hebe. I myself was in the spirit of romance; everywhere I went I saw romance. The gleaming lights on State Street were romantic; I have always sought romance on a lighted street. I have seen romance on Broadway; I have seen romance on State Street, also. I saw romance that evening in front of a bank near Thirty-sixth Place. I was gazing at a young couple of the race to which I belong. The spirit of Cupid was upon them; the spirit of Cupid is very youthful. I am very fond of the youthful spirit; I am fond of everything romantic. Life is on State Street; Life was beckoning me to a very remarkable place of amusement. So I drifted to a spot not far from the other end of the Thirties. I am very fond of that spot wrought with all the splendors of a court in "Arabian Nights." If you want to know the joys of romance seek a carnival on a warm evening in May. If you want to know the romance that lies in the common people seek a carnival on a warm evening in May. If you do this you will regret that there are not more carnivals and more warm evenings in May. The carnival that I saw was like a fairy palace, gaudy in its splendor, riotous in its color, rich in the brotherhood of man and the testimony of what common people think and feel. I am one of the common people and I am certain that you are also one of the common people. Therefore I am

confident that you will enjoy hearing about ourselves.

The first thing that attracted my attention was a Gypsy tent. It was surrounded by several women and several men gazing at a gypsy fortune teller, clothed in the gaudy costume of the romantic Roumanians. A sign in flaring red letters decorated the tent and announced to the spectators that Sophelia the Gypsy Queen could speak in seven different languages and tell everything concerning the past, present and future that is written in the Book of Fate. I have never seen the Book of Fate but I think that if it holds the past, present and future of so many people, it would be impossible to put it in a tent as small as that tent. I am also wondering why it was necessary for a woman to speak in seven different languages when those whose patronage she was seeking could speak in only one language. I was over on the other side of the carnival ground when I ascertained another Gypsy fortune teller. She was also one who talked in seven different languages. I only wish that she had mastered the English language and had been able to tell me when I would be the happiest man in the world. She certainly mastered the arrangement of colors judging from the different hues of the rainbow that were in her costume. She had a young daughter as dark complected as she was, who stood in the doorway of the tent as Minnehaha stood awaiting the coming of Hiawatha. I do not know who her Hiawatha is, but I surmise that he is a dark complected fellow who will come to her as the Indian Hiawatha came to his bride. Perhaps he too will speak in seven different languages the sweet words of the winged god Cupid and win his bride as Hiawatha won the lovely Laughing Water.

Between these Gypsy tents was a Merry-go-Round, that very romantic angel of pleasure, feeding the souls of the weary with the ambrosia of recreation. A merry-go-round appeals to every one because it gives its patrons the opportunity to enter a different world. A merry-go-round is merely a contraption of horses manufactured out of pressed wood, seats that resemble the chariots of the Angels, and music which, despite its mechanical nature lifts one into a plane far different from that of the every day world. I stood enraptured at this merry-go-round, happy to be one who could be in the crowd gazing upon the happiness of those who were riding on the horses and in the seats of the chariots. There was one couple that was of the race to which I belong who had upon them a large portion of the spirit of the winged god. The girl was seated on one of the horses in somewhat the fashion of a Lady Godiva and the young lover was standing beside her gazing into her eyes, as I imagine Othello gazed into the eyes of Desdemona. There was also three young ladies seated on the white horses who reminded me of the three little maidens from school who entertained the court of the Mikado. They were of the race to which I belong and were imbued with all the cheerfulness of a Spring evening.

There were other attractions; but the chief attraction was the crowd of happy carefree people. I imagine that they had laid aside their work, that they had had their evening meal, that they had gone for a stroll up the lighted State Street and attracted by the cheerfulness of the carnival had entered the grounds. I could easily perceive that they were enjoying themselves, that they were meeting those whom they knew and perhaps forming fresh acquaintances. The amusement that gives a person the opportunity to meet another is a worthy amusement. It is interesting to study the crowd; the crowd is the symbol of life. This crowd was laughing sometimes and sometimes very sober. They wore the costumes of an early May but were sometimes brightened by the costume of the light hearted June. They ate peanuts, carried dolls, played little games of chance and stood around one counter that had a large amount of flour and sugar. The sugar was an object of curiosity; many wondered from whence all of that sugar had been obtained. There was enough sugar on that counter to sweeten a dozen cups of coffee or to make one good lemon cream pie.

I might add that there were plenty of lights. A carnival without lights is a failure. You perceive this carnival was a success because it had a very large crowd. A carnival without a crowd is indeed a failure.